Socksie's Adve[illegible]

Book One: Follow Your Heart

Written and illustrated by

Krzysiek Kris Młodzik

Text edited by

Adelle Sesay and Kate Williams

Book design and formatting:

Krzysiek Kris Młodzik

Angel & Dragon Books©

Angel & Dragon Books©

To

Renée & Socksie

Maja & Tiger

Kate &

Rupert + Barny

Adelle &

Mr Mistoffolees

CHAPTER 1

In the garden of a suburbian house, a warm breeze rustled the leaves on the trees which shimmered under the golden rays of the sun.

The garden was home to family of five cats.

"Just look at that one, everybody! Look, look, quickly, before it changes!" Meow Cutie said, pointing at one of the clouds. "It looks like a fish or something like that!"

Her brother Coco laughed.

"I think it rather looks like you. A little silly white sheep."

Coco's fur was ginger and black.

"I told you many times," he said, "that my colours are way cooler than yours."

Meow Cutie looked at him with squinted eyes and started chasing him around the apple tree.

"Children, children, stop arguing," their mum said,
looking around with a frown.
"Hang on a minute. Have any of you seen Socksie?
Where has he gone this time? Coco! Cutie!"
The siblings stopped running, shook their heads at the
same time as if they were one body, and went off again.
"If he doesn't come back very soon, he is going to be in
big trouble," Mama Cat said, paws on hips.
Daddy Cat yawned. He lay on the grass, half asleep.
"I'm sure he is alright," he said.
"I wanted to take you all on a trip today,"
Mama Cat said." It's such a beautiful day. But obviously
we can't go anywhere until we find that little rascal."
Daddy Cat grimaced and, lowering his voice, said:
"Trip? Seriously, in this heat?"

CHAPTER 2

"Here I am, mummy!" Socksie spoke.
He sat on the roof of the house, smiling.
Socksie was the youngest of the family.
With his mostly black fur, white ankles and paws, he looked like he wore socks.
Hence his name.
"Where are we going?!" he said. "How about the woods? I've heard that..."
"I was thinking about a trip to the lake," Mama Cat said.
Socksie frowned and shook his head.
"The lake again?"
He jumped down on to the roof of the wooden shed, then on to the ground and stood next to his mum.
"I've heard that there was something magical happening in the woods," he said looking at his mum.

Mama Cat rolled her eyes.
"And where did you hear of such nonsense?!
We are leaving in five minutes, everybody. I'm not going to wait."
"I am not coming with you!" Socksie said loudly and turned his back to her. "You never like my ideas. You always want to do only what you want, it's not fair!"
He jumped onto the shed and back on to the roof of the house.
"I'm not going to the lake!" he shouted.
"Suit yourself and sit up there if you want! We are not going to ruin everyone's day just because you are such a stubborn, naughty boy! Daddy, why don't you get up and do something? Go and fetch my brother. He can look after this rascal."
Mama Cat's brother, Snowie was the uncle of Socksie and his siblings. His fur was as white as his sister's though that was were their similarities ended. They had completely different views on life and could rarely agree on anything.

She preferred doing things in the way she had always done them. He was the opposite - Uncle Snowie liked daydreaming and considered himself a free spirit. Socksie's mum knew how much her little one loved spending time with his uncle, so despite animosities between her and Snowie she decided that he would be her best bet for looking after the youngest. Especially since he's so grumpy now, she thought.

CHAPTER 3

"So tell me, my dear boy, how have you..." Uncle Snowie began to say to Socksie but in that very moment they heard a noise behind them.

They turned. A cat with shaggy brown and ginger fur sat on the top of the wooden garden fence, breathing loudly.

Snowie's eyes widened and he smiled.

"Socksie, look who's here! Sergio, my very best friend! Are you looking for me? Everything okay?"

"Hi, Snowie," Sergio said slowly. "I'm good, thanks mate. But yes, I've been looking for you everywhere."

"What's the matter, Sergio? Come on, tell me."

"It's the lynx!"

Snowie laughed.

"What? Lynx? What are you talking about?"

Could it be something to do with the woods and the magic that I've heard about? Socksie thought, feeling as though his tummy was full of butterflies.

Sergio jumped off the fence.

Him and Snowie shook paws.

"One of my sister's friends saw a massive lynx heading towards our town," Sergio said.
"I thought you might want to join me. I'm going there now."
Uncle Snowie grimaced and scratched his ear.
"But what is going on?" he said.
"Why such a big deal about some lynx, I don't understand.
Is he dangerous?"
"Come along, my brother, let's find out!
We have not experienced a real adventure for a very long time, have we? Maybe now is the time to change that."
Snowie looked Sergio in the eye.
Then turned to Socksie who nodded vigourously, his green eyes shining and wide open.
"Alright, we're going!" Snowie said.
"I've so missed going on adventures."

CHAPTER 4

Soon after, the three friends reached an area of the town where the busy streets became a narrow road with a few small houses. The landscape consisted mainly of vast fields and meadows that glimmered in the scorching sun, the horizon decorated with a line of trees.

"Is that where he came from, the lynx, Uncle Snowie?" Socksie said, pointing towards the woods.

"Maybe ask Sergio, my boy."

"Mr. Sergio," Socksie said, "is that where the lynx came from?"

Sergio smiled, his head turned towards the horizon.

"That is what I've been told, my friend. Where do you think he will be now, Snowie?"

In that moment they heard a voice coming from behind. They turned. A cat with light brown fluffy fur was quickly approaching them.

Snowie raised a paw.
"Hello, Chatty!" he said.
"Hello there, are you looking for the lynx?"
Chatty said with a grin.
"Actually, yes we are..."
"Good that you've found me then!"
Chatty said with a wry smile.
"Chatty's real name's Chadwick," Sergio said to Socksie.
"He got his nickname because of his tendency to
constantly chat and gossip.".

Chatty narrowed his eyes.
"No gossip, no gossip..."
"Where is he Mr. Chatty?" Socksie said, shuffling from one foot to the other.
"Um, what? Where is who?"
"The lynx! Where's the lynx gone?"
"Oh! Well, he's gone to the old shoe factory. Other cats are already gathering there too, there are lots of them."
"Is he here to show us something magical?! " Socksie said.
"I don't really know, my dear boy but it looks as though he is very friendly. Anyway, got to go! I wish I could come along with you but my wife has just given birth to our four babies, so I need to get back to her now."
"Oh, my congratulations, Chatty!" Uncle Snowie said.
The trio thanked Chatty and began walking towards the shoe factory.
"Don't forget to pop by later and tell me all about it!" Chatty shouted from behind them.

CHAPTER 5

The ruins of the old shoe factory stood in the middle of a field covered with high grass and weeds. Socksie, his uncle and Sergio (with the ease of their feline kind) squeezed through a hole in the wire fence that encircled the grounds.

"This place already feels strange and mysterious," Snowie said, "and we haven't even reached the factory yet!"

"I wonder what that lynx is up to,"
Socksie said in a hushed voice.
"We shall soon find out. Are you frightened?"
Socksie quickly looked away and down.
"Me? No, no, not at all! I'm just, you know, very curious, I guess."
Uncle Snowie smiled and gently patted Socksie's head.
"Don't worry, my boy, you've got me and Sergio.
Nothing's going to happen to you, I promise."
"He can't be that scary," Sergio said,
"if others have come to see him."
Snowie nodded and began to walk. "Let's go gentlemen,"
he said. "Let's finally find out what brings that lynx to our town."
After a few minutes Socksie, panting loudly, said:
"This grass is so high, Uncle Snowie. I'm not sure if I can keep up with you."

Uncle Snowie stopped.
"You can jump on my back if you want. I can see that you are struggling."
"Oh, thank you, Uncle Snowie, that will be great!"
Several minutes later the adventurers reached a specious yard, at the back of which stood the old shoe factory. Cats were already gathered in a circle sitting on the gravel facing the ruins.
"Wow, there's at least twenty of them!" Socksie said.
"And there, in the middle... that must be him! The lynx! He looks really, really old."
"Welcome, welcome, brothers!" The lynx spoke in a booming voice. His fur was light brown with orange and white patches.
"No need to be afraid, come closer and join us."
Socksie, Snowie, Sergio, all looked at one another, then sat behind the gatherers.

"Wow, this is so exciting," Socksie whispered in Uncle Snowie's ear.

"You are all here for a reason," the lynx said, smiled and winked at Socksie. "It is not only because of curiosity that you've come here. Your hearts have been drawn to me today."

Socksie took a deep breath. He felt like his heart was growing bigger. He stared into glowing yellow eyes of the big cat.

CHAPTER 6

"Most of you already know my name," the old lynx said. "I am Ramoon. I've lived in the woods for many many years. Today, the spirits of the woods have asked me to come and visit you and share some of my knowledge."

Socksie's eyes widened, he opened his mouth.

This must be it! He thought. This has to have something to do with that magic I have heard about!

"I am here to help you," Ramoon said. "I bring to you a gift of healing and understanding of your life challenges."

In that moment Socksie felt something he thought he had never felt before. What is happening to me?! It feels very, very strange, like all of this has already happened! But how?! How can I remember Ramoon, all these other cats, our trip with uncle Snowie...

"It was in my dream!" Socksie shouted.

Everyone, including his companions, turned and looked at him.

"Ssshhhh," Uncle Snowie whispered and glanced at the lynx.

Ramoon laughed, then smiling, turned to Socksie.
"Most of us these days think that only things that we can see, touch, hear, smell or taste are real.
Though there's much more to our life than these.
Like our dreams for example, my dear boy.
There is so much magic and energy that is invisible, but it still exists. Many scientists now confirm this.
You can check it for yourself, this knowledge has become widely accessible."
Socksie and everybody present stared at Ramoon with their mouths wide open, their eyes big like saucers.
"Didn't expect this, Snowie, huh?" Sergio said quietly.
"Never heard anything like it."
"It takes willingness and great courage to seek one's truth," the lynx said smoothing out his long thick whiskers.
"Most of us are often afraid to follow our heart desires.
As an example, let's take you, my friend."
Ramoon looked Snowie in the eye.
Me?! Snowie thought, looking around. He felt his heart pounding and his body began to shake.

CHAPTER 7

Ramoon nodded slowly and spoke in a gentle voice:
"You know this very well, because you used to live this way.
The way in which your heart wanted to live.
But then something happened. Others didn't like you because your free spirit reminded them about their hearts which they chose not to follow.
A painful experience.
You wanted to be loved and accepted, we all want that it is a natural desire. The problem is that when others don't accept us and we want so much to be accepted, then we start prentending to be someone different to our true self.
We are even willing to abandon our true nature and soul.
This way we forget about our happiness. Because our true happiness is already inside us. In our hearts."

Snowie felt his eyes welling up and warmth growing in his heart.
How can it be!? How can he know the truth about me? We've never met before!
"As I mentioned earlier, I possess a gift of healing," Ramoon said. "I am able to see things from your past that prevent you from being your true unique self. I come here today to help you understand yourself."
"But how?" Snowie said quietly.
"When you focus on the beauty of life then you will attract more beautiful experiences. And it works the same way when you focus on problems and difficulties. Come closer, my friend."
Uncle Snowie stepped forward, feeling as though there was some magnetic force pulling him closer to Ramoon.
The lynx touched Snowie's head and said to him:
" Follow your heart and embrace all the things you love doing. Free your heart and mind, no matter what others say about your ways. It is your life and only you decide how you want to live it. As long as your intentions and deeds are pure - it is always for the best."

CHAPTER 8

During the next hour all the adult cats, including Sergio, had a chance to experience something similar to what Snowie had experienced. The words that Ramoon used to address each of the cats and their life challenges were slightly different. Because each cat and their life story was unique.

Snowie observed it all whilst laying on the hard, hot gravel.

Someone finally told me that I've been perfectly fine all along, he contemplated, smiling. With all my daydreaming and craving for excitement and adventures!

Socksie lay next to him.

"That must by a wonderful feeling, Uncle Snowie," he said.

"It is, my boy. It truly is!"

Snowie embraced his nephew.

"I am waiting for my turn. I know that he will not forget me."
"He certainly won't, Socksie."
Later, the old lynx slowly walked up to the little kitten.
"I decided earlier," Ramoon said, "that it would be for the best if you could listen to my conversations with adults first. So you could understand the challenges that grown ups face in life."
Socksie nodded vigourously.
"Yes, one day I will become an adult too."
Ramoon smiled.
"Yes, you will. I know that it's not easy to be the youngest of the family. Especially when other family members sometimes treat you as though you are not important. Very often they do that simply because they do not know any other way. But I will tell you more about this on another occasion, because we are going to meet again."
Socksie smiled. "Really?!" he said.
"Yes, absolutely. And now I am going to say something that I would like you to remember. It can help you to understand that things always happen for a reason."

Challenges can be unpleasant but they can also show us that we are more powerful than we give ourselves a credit for."

Socksie felt a wave of warmth in his heart.

"Those around you are going to test you, this is life," Ramoon said. "But as long as you stay true to yourself, you are going to find your true happiness. Like I told your uncle, your happiness lives deep inside of you, not in the paws of others. Remember, no matter how scary it may feel, always try your best to speak what is true to you. Your truth is unique, the same as you are unique. This is the road to living the life of your dreams."

Socksie looked up at the silhouette towering above him. The sun was now directly behind the lynx and Socksie could no longer see Ramoon's big wise eyes. But he could feel all the love and knowledge that the big cat poured over him.

"This is the happiest moment of my life!"

Socksie shouted. Tears falling down his cheeks.

"Thank you so much Mister Ramoon!"

The old lynx winked and smiled, gently touching Socksie's shoulder.

"Oh, you are most welcome, my dear boy. And like I mentioned earlier, we are going to meet again. There is plenty that I have to share with you."

CHAPTER 10

Back in the family's garden, Socksie, his uncle and Sergio lay in the shade of the apple tree.

"How did he know so much about me? And about you, Snowie, and Socksie?! Incredible!" Sergio said.

Snowie laughed.

"He said he had a gift. Like he could read our minds or something like that."

"But how is that even possible?"

"I think that anything is possible, Mister Sergio," Socksie said and started dancing.

"Look at you! That's my boy!" Uncle Snowie said and joined his nephew.

In that moment they heard familiar voices.

"That's my family coming back!" Socksie shouted.

"You look like you've had an excellent time, my dear sister," Snowie said to Mama Cat.

She frowned and narrowed her eyes.

"And what has made you three so cheerful, huh?"

"Yeah, the trip wasn't too bad, actually," Daddy Cat said to Snowie. "Though I could certainly do with a bit of shade now."
Meow Cutie and Coco started arguing about who of the two had enjoyed the day more.
"So what you three have been up to?" Mama Cat asked again..
Socksie lifted up his chin.
"We went to see some magic. Like I told you earlier..."
"Oh, really? Are you still talking about that nonsense?"
"It's not nonsense, mummy. I can prove it to you when you are ready."
"Wait! Snowie, what is this kitten talking about?"
"Please, let him explain," Uncle Snowie said in a calm voice.
Socksie stepped forward and gave Mama Cat big cuddle.
"I am very young, I know, mummy, and it may be pretty tricky and challenging life but I know how important is to follow my heart. My brave and caring heart, full of adventures, excitement and love! I want to tell you now all about our day and amazing adventure we had..."

THE END

OF THE FIRST ADVENTURE

Angel & Dragon Books

Krzysiek Kris Mlodzik was born 1981 in Bielsko-Biala, Poland. He currently lives in England, UK. Krzysiek is a children's book author, illustrator and self thaught, intuitive artist. In his work Krzysiek aims to express a healthy soul-mind-body connection. His stories promote a power of self - awareness as a way to living a conscious, happy and fulfilled life.

More books on Amazon by Krzysiek:

https://www.amazon.co.uk/Krzysiek-Kris-M%25C5%2582odzik/e/B08P3RLNV9

Shirley's Lighthouse: A short story for children who struggle with time away from their grown ups

Cake or Truth?: Cherish Your Uniqueness

Printed in Great Britain
by Amazon